MCR

5.95

ALICIA'S HAPPY DAY

By Meg Starr

Illustrated by
Ying-hwa Hu & Cornelius Van Wright

Star Bright Books
New York

The name Star Bright Books and the logo are trademarks of Star Bright Books, Inc.
Published by Star Bright Books, Inc., New York.
Star Bright Books may be contacted at The Star Building, 42-26 28th Street, Suite 2C
Long Island City, NY 11101, or visit www.starbrightbooks.com.
Printed in China   9   8   7   6   5   4   3   2   1

Paperback edition ISBN 1-932065-06-7 LCCN 2002111165

Hardback edition :
Library of Congress Cataloging-in-Publication Data

Starr, Meg.
  Alicia's happy day / by Meg Starr ; illustrated by Ying Hwa-hu and
Cornelius Van Wright.
      p. cm.
Summary: Alicia receives greetings from her Hispanic neighborhood as she
walks to her birthday party.
  ISBN 1-887734-85-6
  [1. Birthdays--Fiction. 2. Parties--Fiction. 3. Hispanic
Americans--Fiction.] I. Hwa-hu, Ying, ill. II. Van Wright, Cornelius,
ill. III. Title.
  PZ7.S79735 Al 2002
  [E]--dc21
                           2001004142

May you have a day
that's twirly-swirly.

May you hear salsa
and start to dance.

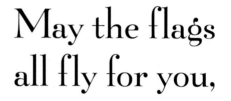

May the flags
all fly for you,

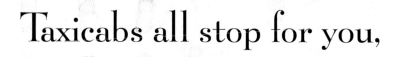

Taxicabs all stop for you,

Airplanes write in
the sky for you,

HAPPY B

Walk signs say
"walk" in time
for you,

And pigeons bow
shiny necks to you,

While friends
decorate in
chalk for you.

May the orange lady give
a ribbon of peel to you,

And the Icey man say,
"Helado de Coco for you."

May Mammi
and Poppi hug
you,

Titi Penelope
sing to you,

Baby Anibal give
his bobo to you.

May you
laugh as loud
as you want,
with no one to
stop you, because
all of us, we're all
for you—that's
why we sing happy
birthday to YOU!

Alicia's Happy Day

Lyrics by Meg Starr
Music by Pepé Castillo

© 2002 Pepé Castillo (BMI)

Music copyright © 2002 Pepé Castillo.

For more information regarding Pepé Castillo's recording of "Alicia's Happy Day," or to order copies of the CD, please contact mmmsrnb@igc.org.